Our Little Arabian Cousin

Blanche Mcmanus

Edition : Culturea (Hérault, 34)
Contact : infos@culturea.fr
Print in Germany by Books on Demand
Design and layout : Derek Murphy
Layout : Reedsy (https://reedsy.com/)
ISBN : 9791041826032
Légal deposit : July 2023

Our Little Arabian Cousin

CHAPTER I

RASHID COMES TO THE BLACK TENTS

"THEY come, father, they come; I see a cloud of dust just over the hills," cried young Hamid, galloping up on his fiery little pony to where his father sat proudly on his horse, with a number of the men of his tribe around him. Al-Abukar, Hamid's father, was a grave, dignified Bedouin Arab, with a flowing beard and a long white cloak completely covering him. In his right hand he held a long lance or spear.

"Nay, nay," said Al-Abukar, shading his eyes with his hand, as he looked out across the desert, "'tis only the sand caught up in a swirl of the wind. Be not impatient, my son," he continued, "thou wilt tire both thyself and the little mare if thou dashest needlessly about, and neither of you will be able to greet thy little friend with the proper spirit."

Hamid and Zuleika, the little pony, both tossed their heads at the idea of such a thing; and no wonder! for Hamid belonged to the Beni-Harb, one of the best and bravest of the Bedouin tribes. As for Zuleika, she had come from the Nijd Desert, where the finest Arabian horses are bred, and it was said she was a descendant of the famous horse of Saladin, the great Arab ruler of olden times.

The pony's coat was rough and shaggy, and not smooth and glossy as we like to see; but Hamid could soon show you all her good points. The small head, with its thin pointed ears, wide nostrils, and large eyes, and the proud arch of her neck and the network of muscles on her wiry legs all showed that she was an Arabian horse of the bluest blood.

Hamid and his father had ridden out into the desert to meet little Rashid, a young friend of theirs who lived in the city of Medina. Rashid had been ill, and it was not easy to get well in the hot, narrow, ill-smelling streets of an Arabian city; so his father was bringing him to stay some months with Hamid, that he might live in a tent and breathe the dry, pure air of the desert, drink plenty of camel's milk, and thus become well and strong.

"The People of the Walls," as the Arabs of the desert call the folk who live in the towns, often send their children to live for awhile in the "Black Tents" in the desert, that they may grow up strong and healthy and become hardy and brave like the Bedouins themselves. The Bedouins, the real desert Arabs, are among the bravest and most courageous people in all the world. The "Black Tents," the habitations of the Bedouins, are so called because they are made of a material very sombre and dark in colour.

"Could we not ride farther out to meet our friends?" asked Hamid, for both he and Zuleika were becoming more and more restless.

"I fear we should miss them, for I know not whether they will come over the ridge or by the road up the valley," said his father.

Just at this moment one of the Bedouins called out: "Do I not see the dust from the camels' feet over yonder?"

"Ah, it is truly they; haste and we will give them welcome." So saying, Al-Abukar spurred his horse forward, and Hamid and his pony were not far behind. Together they flew like the wind over the sand and rocks.

As they came in sight of their friends, they shouted out their names, at the same time throwing their lances into the air and catchingthem again, and firing off their guns in real circus fashion.

You would think that all this would frighten one's friends to death, but this is only the polite Bedouin way of welcoming any one.

The camels of the caravan which was bringing the people from Medina came to a halt and everybody dismounted, and loud and warm were the greetings between friends.

Hamid and Rashid clapped the palms of their right hands together, and then touched foreheads and put their arms around each other's necks. This is the real Arab form of greeting a friend. They are more affectionate than any of the other Eastern nations, and show their joy and happiness with much emotion when meeting friends or relatives.

All now formed one group and rode along together until they came in sight of a grove of palm-trees in the midst of which was Hamid's home, a great brown tent made of cloth of camel's hair, and held to the ground by ropes tightly pegged down so that the strong winds of the desert might not overturn it. All around were the tents of other Bedouins, relatives and friends of Al-Abukar, belonging to the same tribe.

As our party reached the tents, the men and children left behind came forward to welcome them with shouts and more gun-firing.

"Prepare the guest-rice at once," called out Al-Abukar, as he pulled aside the curtains of the tent for his friends to enter. Here was Zubaydah, Hamid's mother, ready to welcome them, and she had the black servant bring a large bowl of water so that they could wash off the dust of travel.

After this all sat around on rugs, and Rashid was made to lie down on a pile of cushions, for he was very tired after his long journey. Fatimah, Hamid's little sister, now brought the guests rose-water with which to bathe their fingers and faces once more, and bowls of water, sweetened with the juice of pomegranates, to drink.

"In the name of Allah, the Merciful!" exclaimed every one, as each took a drink from the bowl; and, after they had finished, "Praise be to Allah!"

"Pleasure and health to thee," said Al-Abukar, politely, as he put his great hubble-bubble pipe before his friend, first taking a puff at it himself.

Meanwhile Hamid was busy pounding coffee, which had been freshly roasted, into a powder, with a mortar and pestle. This is always the occupation of the oldest son when guests are about, the father taking it upon himself to make the coffee afterwards. The Arabs are great coffee-drinkers, and it is from Arabia that the finest mocha comes. It gets its name from a town in the southern part of Arabia.

Al-Abukar made the coffee in a great brass urn, mixing the ground coffee with sweet-smelling herbs. As soon as it was ready for drinking, he himself took the first cup, after which tiny brass cups were filled and passed around to the guests. He did not fill the cups quite full; for that, for some reason, would be a great insult to his guests. Moreover, the cups were so tiny that they held hardly more than the cups of a doll's tea-service would hold. Each emptied his cup twice of the delicious coffee without milk or sugar; but not for anything would Al-Abukar have offered them a third, for that would be deemed a hint that he wished his guests to leave.

Now all the relatives and friends from the other tents came in to call, and sat around smoking and drinking still more coffee, and listening to the gossip of the city and country.

The Bedouins are very hospitable, look upon a guest and his rights as sacred, and are ever ready to avenge a wrong against him. ABedouin will entertain any one who calls at his tent; and, while you are his guest, you will be protected to the utmost power of your host, and treated quite as one of the family. At the same time a stranger is only expected to stay three days; but, when he leaves, his host simply passes him on to another friend or relative, where he may stay another three days. He is welcomed thus by as many of the tribe as he wishes to visit. All very delightful this, you will think; and, if you ever wish to visit your little Arabian cousins, you will always be sure of a warm welcome.

A Bedouin will never harm any one after he has once eaten with him. They call this "eating salt" together; and there are some tribes that expect every stranger they come across to eat with them in order that eternal peace may be assured.

Just now there was a smell of good cooking coming from that part of the tent which was curtained off for the women, and where Zubaydah and the black servants were making all sorts of dishes for the visitors. One of the servants having ground the wheat for the bread between two great stones, it was mixed with milk and bean flour and made into round, flat, thin cakes. Then it was baked in a queer kind of an oven shaped like a big jar with a wide mouth.

Besides these hot cakes, there was to be the "guest-rice," all swimming in melted butter. There was goat's meat, too, of which the Arabs are very fond; but which we would think a little strong to eat often. Curds made of camel's milk were a special feature, and many kinds of soft white cheeses, as well as dates, grapes, and pomegranates.

All these things were put on a great brass tray, which was placed on a low table in the centre of the tent. Every one sat closely around the table, and all said "Bismillah" before eating, which is the Mohammedan way of saying grace.

Al-Abukar helped himself first; and then put a choice bit into his friend's mouth. Then every one began to dip into the dishes with their fingers, because there were no knives or forks or separate plates. They all ate with a good appetite, for there is nothing like the desert air to give one a good appetite.

Zubaydah waited on the guests herself, and afterwards ate with the children, who meantime had been simply looking on.

After the meal was over, they all sat around in a cool corner of the tent, the men smoking their great pipes again. Hamid could not keep his eyes off the beautiful sword and the brace of fine pistols with their red cords, which belonged to his father's friend. They were the most beautiful things he had ever seen, he thought.

Hamid had not a bit of the shyness which Eastern children usually have, for the Arab children are taught from their earliest days always to be independent; and their elders talk with them and encourage them to ask questions. This is a part of their education.

So Hamid was told all about Medina and the doings of the great city; and his father's friend took off his great sword that Hamid might fasten it at his own waist.

"Some day I shall have a sword just like that," said Hamid, as he handed it back, after having marched around the tent with it dragging on the ground behind him. Rashid lay on the soft cushions and laughed, still too tired to get up and rush about as Hamid was doing.

Rashid's father, the Sharif, had brought a gift of a beautiful chased dagger of Damascus steel for Al-Abukar.

"It is indeed a beautiful weapon," said Hamid's father, feeling its polished blade with careful fingers. No gift could possibly please an Arab more than a good weapon, and he thanked his friend from the city again and again.

"Here is also a toy from the bazaar that I have brought thy son," said the Sharif. "See," he continued, "it is a toy camel with a strange device inside its body by which it moves its head and legs. 'Tis one of those strange mechanical toys that are the work of infidels in a foreign land, but all the same none the less wonderful for that." (The Mohammedans call all the people of other faiths infidels.)

"Nay, one needs no toys from the town," said Hamid, proudly. "We play with live camels and horses and chase the wild beasts across the desert."

We would think it very rude indeed of a little boy to speak thus; but instead of scolding Hamid, they praised him; and the Sharif said, smilingly, "Truly thou art one of the 'sons of fight.'" That is what the word Beni-Harb, the name of their tribe, means in the Arabic language.

This is the true Arab spirit; and children are taught to scorn childish things so that they may the sooner become hardy and brave in any kind of danger. It is really very funny to see the little boys act and talk as if they were already grown men like their fathers; and they would much rather play with swords and pistols any day than with toys.

"Indeed thou art a little fighting hawk. May Allah grant that the sweet wind of the desert put strength into the limbs of my son," continued Al-Abukar's guest, looking sorrowfully at little Rashid's pale cheeks as he lay on his cushions.

"He is a little better already," said Zubaydah, kindly, as she gave little Fatimah a censer of burning musk to swing before her guests, that they might enjoy the smell of sweet perfumes after the meal.

"I will show you my falcons if you are not too tired," said Hamid, anxious to amuse his little friend.

"Oh, indeed I am not tired. Where are they?" cried Rashid, jumping up and forgetting all about his long ride.

Hamid led his little guest out among the great palm-trees and past a great many tents to a sort of mud hut thatched with palm leaves.

"How are the birds to-day?" asked Hamid of a man who was sitting in front of the hut, while two fine greyhounds lay beside him. "I have brought a little friend with me who will hunt with the falcons some day."

"May it be soon," said the thin, wiry Bedouin, rising and drawing the curtain of the hut. "The old ones are impatient to be flung to the wind, and I would teach the young ones something more."

This man was Awad, the old falconer, the man who trains falcons, who was only too proud to show off his household of fine birds. These hawk-like birds, called falcons, are great hunters of small game; and can be trained to hunt for their masters, just as one can train a dog. The falcon drops down on its prey from above, in a swift, straight line, and buries its sharp claws in its back, often killing it before its master comes up.

Hamid showed Rashid how he could make his two handsome falcons come and sit on his wrist and obey him. He could throw them off into the air, and they would come back to him when he whistled.

"Some day when thou art stronger, we will go out with the falcons," said Hamid, as he put the birds back on their perch.

When they left the hut, they saw Fatimah running toward them, a dear little gazelle bounding along by her side.

"Isn't she beautiful?" said Fatimah, as Rashid stroked the gazelle's dainty head. "I think falcons are cruel because they chase these pretty creatures. My little pet was caught by the falcons; and, when father brought her home, I begged him to give her to me for a playmate. Now, more than ever, I do not like to have the falcons chase these dear, gentle little animals." Then she put her arms around the gazelle's neck and hugged it.

When the children went back to the tent, they found that the older folk had had their siesta, or midday sleep, and were now sitting in front of the tent.

Zubaydah had the supper-tray brought out to the children; and, when they had again eaten, while the men were sitting around smoking their perfumed water-pipes, the full moon came up over the ridge and made it almost as light as day; for the moonlight of the desert seems brighter than moonlight anywhere else because the air is so clear.

Now they all began to tell stories and recite poetry, of which the Arabs are very fond. The Arab loves to hear and to tell stories about the great deeds of their people in the past, and to recite beautiful poems in praise of the glories of many years ago.

Finally Fatimah brought out her lute, a queer little instrument with only one string, which did not make much music. But the song was very pretty, and Fatimah sang it very sweetly:

"Oh, take these purple robes away,

Give back my cloak of camel's hair,

And bear me from this tow'ring pile

To where the 'Black Tents' flap the air.

"The camel's colt with falt'ring tread,

The dog that bays at all but me,

Delight me more than ambling mules—

Than every art of minstrelsy."

After the song, Rashid and Hamid rolled themselves up in warm blankets in a corner of the big tent and were soon asleep. So ended Rashid's first day in the "Black Tents."

CHAPTER II

HAMID AND RASHID AT PLAY

WHEN little Rashid woke up the next morning, he rubbed his eyes and for a moment wondered if he was dreaming. It seemed so strange to find himself lying in the corner of the big tent instead of in his own room, with his pet doves cooing at his window.

But instead of doves, what he heard was the neighing and stamping of horses, and the calls of the men driving the camels out to pasture. As he turned his head, he found Hamid's mother standing beside him with a bowl in her hand.

"Here is warm milk from the camel," she said, with a smile, "to make thee well and redden thy cheeks. Hasten to drink it while it iswarm. There is water in yonder basin with which to wash," she added.

Rashid was up in a minute, and dashed the water over his face and hands. Then he made his prayer like a good little Mohammedan that he was, for he must do this before eating.

"I never tasted anything nicer than that," said he, as he finished his bowl of milk.

"'Tis good for thee to be hungry, for it means that thou art already better," said little Fatimah, wisely, giving him a piece of the cake which had been baked the night before. She had brought in her bowl to keep him company at his breakfast.

"Where is Hamid?" asked Rashid, looking around for his little friend.

"He has been in and out many times; but I would not let him waken you," said Zubaydah.

"He is full of a secret that he will not tell me," spoke up Fatimah, in rather a hurt voice.

Just then Hamid poked his head in behind the curtain of the tent in a great state of excitement.

"Come, Rashid," he said, "and tell me what thou findest here."

Rashid ran at once out from the tent, and there stood a fine little blooded Arabian horse, all saddled and bridled.

"Oh, what a beautiful little horse!" exclaimed Rashid.

"She only waits for her master," said a voice behind him, and he turned to find Al-Abukar smiling gravely.

"The horse is thine," he said. "She will also help to bring strength to thy limbs, and will carry thee like the wind across the plains and hills."

Little Rashid was so astonished and happy that he could not find words with which to thank his kind friend for his gift, but he kissed his hand and stammered out something. Then he threw his arms about the pony's arched neck and patted her delicate little nose. Oh, how beautiful he thought the handsome red saddle and bridle, with their silver buckles and red tassels! There is no gift that pleases a little Arab boy so much as a fine pony.

"Is she not a queen?" said Hamid, who was as much pleased as his little friend. "I rode with father to the tents of the great Sheik, where one finds the best and swiftest horses; and I helped to pick her out from dozens of other ponies. She belongs to one of the five great families, does she not, father?"

Hamid, like all little Arab boys, had been taught to love horses, and to know the history of the great breeds of Arabia as well as he did that of his own tribe.

"Oh, she knows me already!" exclaimed Rashid, with delight, as the pony rubbed her little nose against his arm.

"She looks lovely and haughty, like a little Sultanah," he continued.

"What shall you call her?" asked Fatimah, who was giving the pony a bit of her cake to nibble.

"I will call her 'Sultanah,'" said Rashid, as he clapped his hands; and everybody agreed that the little horse could not have a better name.

"Now you must feed her, Rashid, so that she will know that she belongs to you," said Hamid. "I will get some of the date bread." He ran back quickly into the tent, and was back again in a moment with a brown, sticky mass in his hand, a kind of paste made of dried dates. This Rashid fed to Sultanah, who seemed to enjoy it very much.

"You must sometimes feed her meat, too; that will make her strong and swift," added Hamid, who was proud indeed to be able to show that he knew all about Arabian ponies.

"Our cousin who lives near the sea gives his horses dried fish to eat," said Rashid.

"That may be well enough for some horses," replied Hamid, "but I give Zuleika dates and milk and cakes. She eats what her master does. Do you not, my beauty?" he said, stroking Zuleika, who had just strolled up to make friends with the newcomer.

Nothing would do but that Rashid must have a ride at once; so Hamid saddled his pony, too, and away went the two boys cantering swift and sure in the morning sunlight.

"We will pass by the madressah, and let the boys see how fine we are," said Hamid.

The madressah was a low shed made of palm-branches where the little Bedouin boys and girls went to school; for even in the desert the children must study their lessons.

When Hamid and Rashid rode up, a number of children were sitting around on the ground, singing out their recitations at the top of their voices, while the school-mistress sat outside sewing.

But they forgot all about their lessons when they spied the new boy, and ran out to greet Rashid and ask him all sorts of questions; and they patted and praised Sultanah and picked out her good points in a very knowing way.

"Oh, thou truant!" said the school-mistress to Hamid, "why art thou not at thy lessons? Always thou hast thy head filled with other things than thy books."

"Nay, teacher, be not cross; to-morrow we will both come; and you will see that I shall bring you a new pupil," said Hamid, as he and Rashid rode away.

"Here is the place where the ponies are kept," said Hamid, riding up to one side of their tent. The boys jumped off their horses and began to unsaddle.

"We will fasten Sultanah, for she is strange yet to her new home," said Hamid, tying the pony's halter to one of the tent ropes. "But Zuleika would never wander from this spot where I place her until I bid her. She will never let any one touch her but me; and, if a stranger tried to mount her, he would soon find himself lying in the dust.

"Zuleika does everything but talk," Hamid went on, for he loved his horse as if she were one of the family. "Sometimes, when the nights are cold, she will come around to the tent curtain and put her head inside and neigh, and then I let her come inside and stand by the fire."

"Now we will make 'kayf' for awhile; for thou hast rushed about enough for one hot morning," said Hamid, throwing his saddle in one corner of the big tent.

Making "kayf" is just a little Arab boy's way of having a good time doing nothing at all but lying on a rug in a cool corner of a tent, or sitting in the shade of a palm-tree.

Rashid was not sorry to rest after the excitement of the morning, so he curled up on one of the mats and was fast asleep in a minute.

"Thou hast promised to show me the young camels," whispered Rashid when Hamid had finished pounding the coffee after the midday meal.

"Come now, then," said Hamid. "Nassar-Ben and his men guard the camel-colts down by the stream."

The two boys went in and out among the brown tents, jumping over the tent ropes rather than taking the trouble to go around, until they found the big herd of camels with a number of baby camels. They were in the river valley, where there was a good crop of coarse, high grass called camel-grass, because it is so coarse that nothing but a camel could eat it.

It was a great herd of camels, some of them eating of the grass and others lying down in the shade; and all around were frisking numbers of little baby camels.

Hamid's father was a Sheik, or captain of a tribe of Bedouins, the real desert tribes of Arabs, who live only in tents in an oasis of the desert.

They had pitched their tents in this particular spot because of its being a very suitable one in which to pasture their camels. The sole wealth of a Bedouin is his flocks and herds and his horse and his firearms; and, of course, his tent and his few simple belongings.

Some of the Sheiks raise horses, others sheep, and others camels. The people of Hamid's tribe lived by raising and selling camels to their neighbours who did not raise them, or to the merchants in the cities and towns.

"Don't baby camels look as if they would break in two?" said Rashid, as they came up to a group of young camels, "their legs are so long and thin."

"Father is going to take some of the colts to sell to the great Sheik who has the fine horses. Perhaps he will let us go with him," said Hamid. "I heard Nassar-Ben tell him last night that the young camels were now strong enough for the journey.

"Nassar-Ben is our camel-sheik; and he and his men guard the herd. There he sits in the shadow of the tent, and those are his children scrambling around and playing on that old camel's back," continued Hamid, bound that his little friend should know all about everything.

"Wait, oh, babies! I can mount quicker than that," shouted Hamid to Nassar-Ben's children, who were amusing themselves climbing over the back of one of the old camels.

"Look! This is the way to mount a camel," said Hamid, as he climbed up one of the legs of a big camel as if it were a tree-trunk; and, finally, throwing his leg over the beast's neck, he was soon perched on the hump in the middle of the camel's back.

"Come up, come up, that's the stairway!" he called to Rashid.

"Oh, I daren't," cried poor little Rashid, slipping back as he tried to hold on to the camel's rusty knee.

"You will learn in time, my little master," said Nassar-Ben, lifting him up beside Hamid. Then all the other little children swarmed up the old camel's legs; and, when the camel man gave her a blow with a stick, away she went, the children laughing and holding on to each other to keep from slipping off. Suddenly the old camel wheeled around and started back at a gallop. Little Rashid had ridden on a camel before, but never on a bare-back camel in that fashion. The first thing he knew he was lying in the dust, together with one of the little Bedouin boys, whom he had pulled off with him as he fell.

"Oh!" said the little boy, half-crying, "you made me fall off on purpose!" He felt so badly that he, one of the boys of the camel-sheik, should have been seen to fall from a camel that he began to thump Rashid as hard as he could.

"Fie! for shame!" cried Hamid, rushing up to them as he jumped down from the camel. "Is this the way to treat a stranger and a guest in our tents?"

The little boy stopped at once and hung his head, looking very much ashamed; for he knew how wrong it was to be rude to a guest.

"This greenhorn from the town made me fall, and they jeered at me," he said, sulkily.

"Nay, but I did not mean to pull you off," said Rashid; "thou must blame the steep hump of the camel." He looked so sorry that the little fellow stopped frowning at once. They made friends again, and all ran back for another ride on the camel, while Rashid made uphis mind that he would learn to climb and mount a camel all by himself.

After a few days, Rashid's father had to go home, and Rashid had quite a lump in his throat as he sat on Sultanah one morning and watched his father's little caravan pass out of sight over the ridge. He would not have cried for anything, however; and, when he thought of his good friends here in the "Black Tents" and his little pony and the good times he was to have, he felt better.

What with drinking camel's milk and galloping over the plain on Sultanah's back, Rashid soon began to grow strong and well. His little white face changed to a healthy brown colour.

Rashid and Hamid helped the falconer look after his birds, and Awad, their keeper, showed them how to train a falcon oneself.

One day as the boys were sitting under the shadow of a group of big palm-trees playing a sort of "jack-straw" game with date seeds for stones, Rashid suddenly exclaimed: "What can that be?" A sudden flash of light had made his eyes blink, and straightway there was another. "Who is playing tricks?" said Hamid, looking around. Then they heard a low laugh, and there was Fatimah behind a tree, holding a little looking-glass in her hand so that it would flash a ray of sunlight right in the boys' eyes.

"Oh, you monkey! Where did you get that glass, and who is this stranger?" asked Hamid; for he had just spied another little girl's head peeping over Fatimah's shoulder.

"There is a merchant at the great tent. He is Hajj and this is his little granddaughter; and, oh! he has such beautiful things to sell, mirrors like this and silks and jewelry and—but you should see them yourselves!" said Fatimah without stopping for breath.

Hamid did not need to be told the second time. It was a great event in the lives of the desert children whenever a travelling merchant came; for this was the only chance they ever had to buy anything whatever known to the town dwellers.

The children found the old merchant opening up his saddle-bags and spreading his wares on a rug in front of the tent, while everybody crowded around to look at the velvet purses, the silk veils, and trinkets of all kinds as well as weapons and firearms which he displayed.

What caught Hamid's eyes first were the long pistols with funny curved handles set with mother-of-pearl and silver.

"Oh, father!" he said, "thou hast promised me a new pistol! You remember; it was when I shot to the centre of the mark a month ago."

"Ah, thou hast a good memory; but thy mother wants a silken veil and Fatimah some gewgaws," said old Al-Abukar.

"Here is a fine pistol which will just suit the little Sheik," said the old merchant, taking from his own belt a fine weapon, all set with pearl and silver. "This was made for the son of a great prince; but it came to me in the course of trade and it is a gift that will make the boy glad."

"Oh, father! What a beautiful weapon! It will be a long time before one sees such another," exclaimed Hamid, as he handled the weapon lovingly.

"Ah, well," said his father, "a promise is a promise; and one might as well spend the money now as at another time." Then he began to unroll the long sash around his waist, so that he could get at his leather belt in which he kept his money.

Wasn't Hamid a proud boy when he stuck the pistol in his sash and strolled up and down in front of the other boys. They were all envious, too, in a proper way; for it was not every one who could carry a pistol made for a prince.

"Now let us see what thy new pistol will do," said Al-Abukar, taking a coin from his pouch, and, through a hole in it, attaching a string and suspending it from the end of a pole which projected from one side of the tent. He paced backwards a short distance, and told Hamid to stand on that spot and shoot at the string which held the coin and try to cut it with the bullet from his pistol.

"Oh, father, thou hast given me a hard task," said Hamid, as he took his place and began to load his pistol.

"So much the more honour to you if you do it well, then," replied his father. "Aim carefully and not too high," he continued.

Hamid shot at the coin several times, but with no luck.

"Let Rashid try his skill," said Al-Abukar.

Rashid's hand shook as he took aim, and his first shot went wild; but his second just grazed the coin and sent it swinging to and fro like a pendulum.

"Well done! oh, son of the city!" cried out the children from the other tents, who had crowded around to watch the shooting.

Their praise pleased Rashid, for he had practised hard with Hamid at shooting at a mark since he had been in the desert.

"I will do it this time," said Hamid, as he set his teeth. Again, however, he only sent the dust flying about an astonished camel, who just at that moment poked his inquisitive nose out from behind the tent.

"Enough powder and shot has been wasted for one day," said Al-Abukar, raising his pistol; "we will take the coin down." Then, firing at the cord with a sure and steady aim, he cut it as if with a knife.

"It is not the fault of the new pistol," said Al-Abukar, smiling at Hamid, who looked very disappointed. "Never mind, thou wilt succeed better another time," he added.

CHAPTER III

THE ROBBER BAND AND AN OSTRICH HUNT

MEANTIME Fatimah was making friends with Nawara, the old merchant's little granddaughter. She was a wild, shy little girl, wearing a dark blue cotton dress, a mass of tangled black hair hanging down on her shoulders. The hot sun and the wind had burnt her face almost black. She was telling Fatimah of her long journeys with her grandfather.

"Thou art a great traveller," said Fatimah, looking at the little girl in round-eyed wonder.

"Yes, my father and mother are dead," she said, "and, as I have no little brothers or sisters, I go always with grandfather. He makes a nice seat for me on top of the big bales of goods on the camel's back, or he holds me before him on his dromedary."

"And art thou never afraid?" asked Fatimah.

"Oh, no! Sometimes, though, at night, when I hear the jackals howling near our tent, I pull the rug up over my head. But when we come to the 'Black Tents' every one is so kind. I find many little playmates; and often they want me to stay with them. Grandfather would miss me sadly if I did," said Nawara, with an important air. "When we halt I always gather the dry thorns and make the fire, and melt the milk balls to make a cool drink while the cakes are cooking," she went on.

"Thou art indeed quite a little woman," said Fatimah's mother, smiling at the little girl's talk.

"'Tis good to be here," said the merchant, after his other customers had gone and the family had gathered for the evening meal in front of the tent. "We came a long, weary way to-day. I feared to stop by the road, for there was talk of robbers hiding in the hills, and a party of travellers had been attacked by them a few days ago."

"Perhaps we will see them to-morrow, father, and then I will have a chance to use my new pistol," spoke up Hamid, eagerly.

"The rascals give no one a chance to see them. They keep themselves safely hid behind the rocks, and fire upon the peaceful traveller before he is aware that they are there," the merchant replied.

"It is their way," said Al-Abukar. "I would not hasten thy going," he continued; "but if thou wilt join our party we will ride together as far as the tents of our friends. It will be safer for thee and the little one as well as thy goods," said the Sheik.

So it was arranged that the old merchant and Nawara should start out with them the next day.

Hamid and Rashid lay awake half the night, planning what they would do if they met the robbers; and they were up and had saddled their horses while it was yet starlight, so as to get a good start before the heat of the day came down upon them.

The camel men were ready with the camels tied together in a long line, one behind the other, so that they might not stray apart.

The old merchant seated himself cross-legged on his dromedary, which is much like a camel except that it is swifter and has two humps on its back instead of one.

"Thou hast been very kind," said little Nawara, putting her arms around Fatimah and kissing her as they were leaving.

"Thou wilt come again some day, perhaps," said Zubaydah, the mother. "Meantime here is something to keep thee from having to cookthe midday meal," she said, as she stuffed some fresh dates and cakes into the food-bags.

Now the men started the camels, Al-Abukar and the boys swung themselves into their saddles, and away they galloped.

Hamid looked very fine indeed, for a little Bedouin boy likes to look at his best when he is making his first visit. He had put on his long white cloak of camel's-hair cloth, and thrown over his white cap a silk cloth like a large handkerchief with long red tassels at the corners. This was held on by a cord of brown wool wound round and round his head. In the broad silken sash at his waist was stuck a small dagger with a curved blade and of course the new pistol, and his jacket was embroidered with a silver thread.

Rashid, too, was dressed in Bedouin style; and each of the boys carried a spear, while they had polished as brightly as possible the silver buckles and ornaments on their bridles and saddles. To the boys' great disappointment nothing happened and they reached the tents of their friends safely enough. Here they spent three happy days.

While Al-Abukar and his friend the Sheik bargained over the prices of the colts, Hamid and Rashid played with the children of the encampment, riding races on horseback and having a good time generally. Indeed they were sorry when they came to say good-bye, and turned their horses' heads homewards.

"I don't believe there are any robbers, after all," said Rashid to Hamid, as they were riding back together a little ahead of the party.

"They are only men from the mountains, anyway," said Hamid, with a toss of his head, a Bedouin's way of saying he didn't think much of their bravery.

"Some of them are courageous enough," said one of the camel men who had just come up behind them; "and this is just the sort of a place they would choose to lurk in," he continued, looking carefully about him as they entered a ravine between the hills.

Just as the camel man had finished speaking, Hamid looked up and saw a curl of white smoke coming out from behind a rock on the hillside above them.

"Down!" cried Hamid, pushing Rashid forward on his pony's neck and at the same time throwing himself flat on Zuleika's neck just as a bullet went whizzing over their heads.

"'Tis they! the rascals! They are skulking behind the rocks, and will not come out and fight in the open like brave men," cried Al-Abukar, galloping up furiously and sending a shot back in the direction from which they had been attacked.

"Give your horses their rein, boys, and ride on as fast as ever you can. These worthless fellows will have no horses that can overtake yours. I will teach the brigands what it means to fire on a Bedouin chief." So saying, Al-Abukar dashed straight up the rocky side of the ravine.

"I will not flee! I will follow you, father!" cried Hamid, spurring Zuleika on close behind his father's horse. Rashid followed, not knowing what might happen, but determined to stay by Hamid at any cost.

The horses needed no spur, for the sound of the shot had made them wild, and they bounded up the steep rocky trail like gazelles.

The band of robbers were so taken aback at this sudden return of their attack that they fled without a parting shot, but not before Al-Abukar had captured their chief.

"Aha! Thy beard is now in my grasp," said Al-Abukar to the robber chief, as he and his men fastened their prisoner on the back of one of the camels.

"Thou didst not think any one could reach thee on that steep mountainside, but thou didst not reckon on the mettle of the horses of our tribe."

"Look you," said the camel man, as he rode up alongside the boys again, "it was a good thing that you sheltered yourselves behind your horses' necks. Here, Rashid, is the hole of the bullet right through this head-kerchief of yours, and if you had not pulled your little friend down on to his horse's neck as you were riding beside him, Hamid, the bullet would certainly have gone straight through his head."

"Oh, Hamid, you have saved my life," said Rashid, turning pale for the first time. He had been too much excited before to be frightened.

"He only did his duty to his friend," Al-Abukar replied, gravely; but Hamid saw by his look that he was proud of his son. He sat up a little straighter in his saddle and felt that he had grown at least a couple of inches taller during the morning.

"Thou hast disobeyed me, child, but I cannot scold thee," continued his father; "for you and Rashid both followed me like brave little sons of the desert."

"But, father!" said Hamid, clutching at Zuleika's rein, suddenly, "I forgot all about firing my new pistol!" At this they all laughed heartily.

"Never mind," said his father; "I am sorry to say there are still many robbers left, and that you may yet have a chance to use it."

When they rode up to the tents with their prisoner, the robber chief, every one hurrahed; and the mother and Fatimah had, of course, to hear all about the adventures at once.

"Shall we go out to-day, my young masters, and see if we can bring home some hares for our dinner, or perhaps catch a grouse or two?" asked Awad, the falconer, when Hamid and Rashid came to look at the birds on the morning after the adventure with the robbers.

"Yes, indeed!" cried both the boys in one breath; and it was not long before they were speeding over the plain beside Awad, with the two greyhounds leaping along after them.

Awad carried his falcon, and Hamid had his own bird, too, perched on his wrist. Every now and then the boys, out of sheer fun, would throw their spears up in the air and catch them again as they were riding furiously across the plain. This is quite a feat, as you may imagine, when one is riding at full speed, but Hamid could do it easily. His spear was a long bamboo cane with a brass tip on one end, and on the other an iron spear sharpened so that it could be stuck upright in the ground if need be. Next to his pony and his pistol, Hamid was more fond of his spear than of any other of his belongings; and he could not be induced to part with it at any time.

Over the rocky, sandy ground they rode, and through thickets of acacia and mimosa trees. Just as they came out into the open again there was a whirr, and up rose a bevy of birds just in front of them.

"Now is thy chance! Whistle off thy falcon!" cried Awad.

Quick as a flash Hamid threw off his falcon from his wrist, and like a dart it swept after the fleeing birds.

"Ho! my beauty, faster! faster! faster!" cried Hamid, and, patting his pony's neck, he flew along, with Rashid close behind.

"She gains on them!" cried Rashid. Just then the falcon with a shrill cry came up with the poor bird it had been chasing, as it fluttered to the ground tired out; and, fixing its great talons in the feathers of its back, carried it toward Hamid.

"Well done!" cried Awad, as Hamid rode up to him, glowing with pride. "Thou art indeed an apt pupil, and some day will excel thy teacher."

"But thou didst not throw off thy own falcon," said Hamid.

"Nay, I wanted you to have all the glory this time," answered Awad, with a smile. "But now comes my turn," he exclaimed, as he sent his falcon flying after some hares which were scuttling along the ground to their holes. The greyhounds bounded after the frightened little animals; but, though they are the swiftest dogs known, the old falcon which Awad had been carrying on his wrist was faster than they. He caught up with the hares before they did and pounced upon one of them.

By this time the sun was high above the horizon; and the very air seemed quivering, it was so hot.

"We will stop now and have something to eat, this seems a likely place," said the old falconer, as they halted under a tree. The boys declared they were quite ready, and vaulted at once from their horses; for they had eaten only a bit of dry bread before starting out.

"Thrust your spear into the ground, Rashid, as I have mine," said Hamid; "and we will make a tent under which to rest, by hanging Awad's great cloak between them."

"Look, Hamid, what a pretty round, white stone I have found here," called out Rashid, as the end of his lance struck something hard in the sand.

"Stone!" said Hamid, brushing the sand away. "It's an ostrich's egg, and here is another; why, it's an ostrich's nest!"

"Oh, and to think that I found it!" cried Rashid. He had seen the eggs for sale in the bazaars of Medina, and knew that the ostriches bury their eggs in the hot sand, which hatches them out in time; but he had hardly hoped to be able to ever find a real ostrich's nest himself.

"What is this?" asked Awad, as he came up from hobbling the horses. "Ostrich eggs! Then likely enough the bird itself is not far off," he continued, looking around.

"Yes, there she is," cried Hamid, pointing to a spot some distance away. Sure enough, there was the ostrich, with its head buried in the sand.

"Foolish bird! she thinks that as long as she hides her head in the sand, and cannot see us, that we are not able to see her, and that she is safely hidden from danger. Come, let us give chase," said Awad, running back to the horses. So, forgetting the heat and their hunger, the boys jumped on their horses again, while the greyhounds, hot on the scent, led the chase after the big bird.

The ostrich apparently heard them coming and got her head out of the sand quickly enough. And did not the long-legged bird give them a chase, covering yards of ground at each step!

"She is throwing stones at us," laughed Hamid, as the bird's big feet sent a shower of small stones flying back at them.

"Oh, if I only had a stout rope with me," said Awad.

"It is here," said the black servant who had accompanied them, drawing a coil from his saddle-bag and throwing it to Awad as they all galloped onward.

But if the bird was swift, so were the others, too; and, as the greyhounds gained on her, the ostrich grew bewildered until finally she turned at bay and showed fight.

"Beware!" shouted Awad, as he caught Zuleika's bridle and reined her back just as the bird lifted her great foot to strike at Hamid. "A blow from her foot would be a dangerous thing," he continued. At the same time he threw a noose of rope and skilfully entangled the ostrich's foot just as one of the greyhounds sprang at the bird. After many struggles, the ostrich was thrown and secured in spite of its vicious kicks.

Awad sent the servant in hot haste back to the tents to fetch help to get the ostrich home; for it is no easy matter to manage one of these great strong birds, even after you have got it well secured.

At last our little hunting-party had a chance to rest; and, while they ate their dried dates and cakes, the boys talked of nothing but their ostrich hunt. Rashid was sure that this was the most wonderfully interesting day he had ever spent.

CHAPTER IV

RASHID GOES HOME

IN time Awad had trained the ostrich so well that the children could play with her as they did with the camels and ponies.

One day there was a great laughing and shouting around the tents. No wonder! for there came the ostrich stalking along with Hamid and Rashid on her back. Hamid sat astride the bird's neck, guiding it by a rope which was tied around its head for a bridle.

"Let me get up, too," cried Fatimah, who came running out of the tent; and good-natured Awad swung her up beside the boys.

"Hold on tight," he called out, as away went the big bird with a troop of little Bedouin children following a long way after. Such a ride as the children had! Poor Awad was quite breathless when they got back, from running to keep up with the bird's long strides.

But now Rashid's happy days in the desert were coming to an end; for the time had come when he must leave the "Black Tents" and go home. He was well and strong now, and a messenger had come from his father, saying how much he missed his boy, and how all at home wanted to have him back again.

"Oh, Rashid, must you go?" asked Hamid, who felt very sad at losing his little friend.

"Yes, but my father has sent word that you must come back with me, Hamid, for a visit with us."

And so it was all arranged that not only Hamid was to go with Rashid, but all the family as well. Everybody was very busy making preparations.

There were a great many things to do in order to get ready for the journey, for when a Bedouin travels he takes his house and all his belongings with him.

Long before the peep of day Nassar-Ben had his great camels kneeling before the tents, and the camel men began to fasten the loads on the camels' backs, the beasts were groaning and moaning as they always do when they are being loaded. Camels are very cunning and wise, and try to make out that they have already too much to carry, even before they have made the attempt. Every once and awhile they would get up, and the camel men would cry out to them to kneel down again and keep quiet, giving a sharp blow with the curved stick which the drivers always carry to guide the camels.

One of the camels carried a litter in which Fatimah and her mother were to ride. It was like a broad seat and long enough so that Zubaydah and Fatimah might use it as a bed to lie down upon as well. Arched over it were poles on which hung curtains to keep out the dust and sun.

"Isn't this nice and snug?" laughed Fatimah.

"Too snug when all of you little ones are here," answered her mother.

The children had all climbed up into the litter to see just what it was like; and, of course, they had got in the way of Zubaydah who was hanging the pouches or bags around inside the curtains. These contained the food and other necessaries for the journey.

"It is very well for thee, Fatimah, but I am glad I am going to ride Zuleika," said Hamid, slipping out and stopping to watch two men swing two large jars of water across the camel's back behind the litter, which the Arabs called the "shugduf."

All the little Bedouin children of the neighbourhood crowded around to bid Rashid good-bye, for they had grown very fond of him and were sorry to see him go. Each had brought him some little parting gift, such as a string of dates, a bunch of feathers for his spear, or a tame bird.

After Rashid had thanked his kind little friends, there was great fun stowing the presents away so that they might be carried safely, especially the shell of one of the ostrich's eggs which Awad had brought him. Finally Fatimah found a place for this last gift by putting it in a palm-leaf basket and hanging it from the roof of the "shugduf."

At last all was ready. The boys mounted their ponies and the camel men cried out orders to the great beasts, and the camels got up slowly, groaning under their big loads. Al-Abukar looked splendid as he rode at the head of the little caravan on his swift dromedary. Over the dromedary's back were two big saddle-bags with long crimson tassels which hung nearly down to the ground; the saddle itself was of red leather with a high metal pommel at the front and back. Beside the dromedary cantered the two boys.

Rashid turned around and waved a last good-bye with his spear to all his friends whom he had left behind at the encampment, while all the little Bedouins ran after him a little way, shouting at the tops of their voices: "May your shadow never grow less, O little Son of the Walls!"

Soon the "Black Tents" were left far behind, and the camels struck into their regular caravan gait, rolling and lurching like a ship at sea.

If you were riding a camel for the first time you would understand why the Arabs call the camel "the ship of the desert," for it rolls backwards and forwards and pitches first forward and then backward exactly like a ship in mid-ocean.

At noon they halted for the midday meal. While the men hastily put up a tent, the children gathered dry branches in the thickets of thorn-bushes with which to make the fire. Meanwhile Hamid had spied some tents in the distance; and, near them, a woman tending goats.

"May we go and ask her to give us some milk, mother?" asked Fatimah.

"Yes, and here is some bread to give her in exchange for the milk," said Zubaydah.

The Bedouin woman gladly filled the bowl that the children brought with them with nice warm goat's milk, but when Fatimah offered her the bread, she shook her head angrily.

"Nay, nay, I am not a 'labban,'"—a milk-seller,—she said. The true Bedouins think it is a disgrace to sell milk, and that it is only right that they should give it freely to any stranger who may ask for it.

When the children got back with the milk, Zubaydah was frying dates in butter, and soon they were all sitting in the shade of the tent eating heartily of them and the cold meat and rice and cakes.

"The camels are glad to rest, too," said Rashid, watching them as they slowly knelt down one by one. It is one of the funniest sights in the world to see a camel lay down on the ground. He sighs and groans and slowly unbends his funny long legs that look as if they would come unjointed and drop off. He folds up his fore legs a little, then he folds up his hind legs in part, and then he falls on his knees until his nose nearly touches the ground. Now he finishes the folding up process with all his legs, as if they were the blades of a jack-knife, and tucks them well away beneath him.

When it became cooler our party broke camp, and the little caravan started off again over the desert. They passed more and moretents and herds, and also a little party of travellers like themselves, and all shouted salaams, or greetings, as they went by.

When they stopped for their supper, Hamid and Rashid, instead of washing themselves as usual, poured sand over their faces and hands in place of water. This is the Mohammedan custom when travelling in the desert, for where water has to be carried with one, it must not be wasted.

When bedtime came the children were quite ready for it, for it had been a long, hard day. Fatimah said she would rather sleep in the tent; but the two boys rolled themselves up in their rugs on the warm sand outside, and, with their saddles for pillows, slept as soundly as did their ponies, who were tethered beside them.

"Fasten the curtains of the litter well," said Al-Abukar when the little party started off the next day, "the 'poison-wind' has begun to blow."

"Ugh! and it is as hot as if it blew from a furnace," said Hamid, tying the end of his kerchief tightly across his mouth. Rashid did the same, while Fatimah helped her mother to draw the curtains tightly around them; for the simoon, as this great desert wind is called, was blowing great whirls of sand into their faces.

"Here comes a thing of ill-omen," said Hamid's father, pointing to a great column of sand which whirled by them at a rapid rate.

"Ay, it is a genie, the evil spirit of the desert," muttered the old camel-sheik, wrapping his cloak more closely about him.

The genie is practically a pillar of sand drawn up into the air by the wind as it whirls and blows around and around with a circular motion, very much in the same way that a water-spout is formed at sea. The Arabs are all afraid of the genie, and say it is an evil spirit; and no wonder, for these moving columns of sand do not look unlike some strange, living thing as they go dancing across the desert.

The wind was blowing so hard when they halted at midday that they could not think of putting up a tent or cooking; but ate as best they could huddled up beside the kneeling camels, with their cloaks pulled up over their heads.

"I am eating more sand than bread," said Hamid, with disgust, as he held tightly to his cloak to keep it wrapped closely about him, and tried to eat at the same time.

"I know I must have eaten a basketful," said Rashid.

"Oh, there goes my veil," cried Fatimah, who had thoughtlessly popped her head out of the litter.

"Thou wilt never see it again," said her mother. Almost immediately it had been lost to view as it went sailing through the air.

"Never mind, thou shalt buy the prettiest that can be found in the Bazaar when we get to the city," said her father, consolingly.

The little caravan struggled against the wind all the rest of the day; and that night there was no sleeping in a tent for anybody. The next day, however, things went better.

"Oh! I see over there a beautiful lake of blue water and palm-trees beside it," cried Fatimah. "Look, mother," she said, waking her mother from a doze and pointing across the sandy plain.

"Indeed it looks as though there were water and trees ahead," said her mother; but Al-Abukar answered: "Nay, it is but a mirage."

"But we can see the ripple of the water; it must be real," persisted Fatimah.

"Nay," said the camel man, and shielding his eyes with his hand, he peered at the strange sight. "The camels say nothing," he continued, "and they are wise and can always tell when water is near. If it were real water they would begin to whine and groan." Sure enough, as they went toward the mirage, it faded away altogether, the lake, trees, and all.

"But it did look real, did it not, father?" said Fatimah.

"Ah, so has thought many a poor traveller to his undoing, when he was lost in the desert and was dying of thirst," answered her father. "He thinks he sees cool water and green trees ahead of him, and hurries along to reach them, only to find that the mocking mirage has faded away and that there is nothing there but the hot sand of the desert."

A mirage really is nothing more than a sort of reflection of some very distant object projected into the sky through the hot, dry air of the desert. Sometimes the desert traveller sees a phantom city in the clouds, and sometimes a ship, as if it were floating on the sandy waves of the desert instead of on the ocean; but it is all a delusion and not real.

From now on, the little Bedouins began to remark that they were leaving the desert behind them. They began to pass some houses, and then small villages of mud huts with roofs of palm-leaves. Around these villages were little fields divided off by low ridges of earth. There were orchards of fruit-trees, and Hamid and Rashid rode up to one of these and bought some pomegranates.

"Did ever anything taste nicer?" said Fatimah. And they all agreed with her as they ate the sweet, pink pomegranate seeds.

Soon they were riding through great groves of date-palms, and shortly caught a glimpse of the city shining white through the trees still some distance away.

"Oh, Hamid! I believe that is my father yonder," cried Rashid, as he caught sight of several horsemen riding toward them.

It was true; it was the Sharif, Rashid's father, who, with a party of relatives, had come out to meet them. Rashid galloped forward, and in another moment was in the arms of his father.

The caravan came to a halt, and, after many greetings on all sides, got under way again, and they all rode together into the city.

"Is not the big city a wonderful place?" whispered little Fatimah to her mother as they rode through the great city gates of stone, the walls of which were painted with broad bands of yellow and red. She had never before seen a large city.

"Keep clear of the sides, O camel men!" shouted out Nassar-Ben, who had hard work guiding his little caravan through the narrow, winding streets. The camel men had to run behind their charges, prodding them with sticks and crying out: "Go in the middle of the road! O! Hé! O! Hi!"

Finally they came to the great square called the "Kneeling Place of the Camels," because all the caravans which came into the city were obliged to unload or encamp there. On one side of the square was the house in which Rashid lived. "Welcome to our house," said the Sharif, as he led his friends through a gateway and into a large courtyard.

Here they dismounted. Rashid's mother and his big brother, Ali, and all the other relations and servants rushed out to meet them. And wasn't Rashid glad to see them all again!

CHAPTER V

HAMID AND FATIMAH SEE THE GREAT CITY

"WHAT is that?" asked Hamid, who was awakened in the morning by the sound of a voice shouting, "Great is Allah!" He and Rashid were sleeping on the roof of the house, as city Arabs often do in the hot weather.

"That is the 'Muezzin,'" replied Rashid. "Come to the parapet and you can see him."

Rashid pointed to a tall, slender tower not far away. Near the top was a small balcony, on which a man was standing. He calls out these words every day at sunrise and sunset to remind the people that they must not forget to say their prayers. In a monotonous sing-song voice he calls: "Great is Allah! there is no God but Allah and Mohammed is his Prophet." When the people hear this cry, they rise and say their prayers, always looking toward Mecca, the Holy City.

Hamid could see five of these long needle-like towers or minarets, and a great green dome, rising above the tree-tops not far away.

"That is the great Mosque," said Rashid; "and we are going there to-day because— " but he got no further, for just at that moment a dozen or more pigeons came flying about him, fluttering their wings on his face and perching on his shoulders.

"Oh, what pretty birds! How tame they are!" said Hamid, stroking the smooth wings of one of the white doves.

"They are my pets," said Rashid. "They come every morning to be fed. Let us give them their breakfasts." Leading the way to the storeroom on the ground floor, he filled a basket with grain which he took from one of the great bags which were always stored there. Then they scattered the grain all about the courtyard in the centre of the house, to the great delight of the pigeons.

The little Bedouins were eager to see the city; and, of course, the first place that Rashid showed his friends was the great Mosque, as their church was called.

It was the same where Hamid had seen the "Muezzin" in the tower. This Mosque is very sacred to the Arabs, and they visit it at every opportunity, because it is the tomb of the great Arab Prophet Mohammed. When they reached the Mosque, they left their slippers outside, and, after saying a prayer or two, Rashid showed Hamid and Fatimah around the great building.

After this they walked down the long street that led from the Mosque to the great City Gate. Here were gathered all the shops. Such funny little shops! Nothing but little rickety wooden booths thatched with palm-leaves, and very dingy and dirty. However, they contained many wonderful and curious things. The children marvelled at them all. There were great strings and bunches of pink, red, and white coral that is found on the rocks in the Red Sea, and there were ornaments and jewelry made of mother-of-pearl; as well as many kinds of strange weapons, whose handles were inlaid with pieces of this same glittering shell.

"Just look at that lamp," said Hamid, "made from an ostrich's egg," as he stopped before one of the booths where the shells of the eggs of these big birds had been mounted in brass and silver and made into hanging-lamps, pipe-bowls, and vases.

Fatimah was very happy. She had found a booth where she could buy a pretty rose-coloured veil to replace the one she had lost in the desert.

In the shadow of the big City Gate a number of children were sitting weaving baskets and mats of palm-leaves.

"How easily she does it," said Fatimah, as they stood watching one of the little girls plait the long strips of dry leaves into a pretty basket.

By the time our little party had walked up and down the long line of shops many times, they were quite ready to go home and rest in the balcony of the "majlis," or parlour of the house. The children soon found that this balcony was a very cosy nook in which to sit because it hung out over the street, so that they might easily see everything which went on in the big, lively square.

The "majlis" itself, which extended back into the house, was a great big, bare room with a divan of cushions around the walls and a large rug covering the floor in the centre. There was no furniture except a low table in the middle, on which were the hubble-bubblepipes and a brass tray which held the coffee-pot and cups. High up on the wall hung some swords and guns well out of the reach of the little folks.

Some days later Hamid was kneeling in the "majlis" balcony and peeping out through the carved wooden lattice which enclosed the balcony on the street side, while Fatimah stood behind him looking over his shoulder. Suddenly Rashid put his head in at the door and exclaimed: "I have been looking everywhere for thee."

"Just come and look out on the square, Rashid; it is full of people and camels and horses, and tents are being put up all over it," called out Hamid.

"It is the big caravan that comes from Damascus. They are the pilgrims on their way to the Holy City," said Rashid, joining them on the balcony. "I was looking everywhere for thee to tell thee of it. Father says there are many thousands of the pilgrims."

Such a bustle and scurrying about and noise as there was in the big square. Tents were being put up like magic, camels were being unloaded, and horses and donkeys and dromedaries were stamping around, and little children were tearing about everywhere and getting in the way,—for many of the pilgrims take their families with them.

"There are the tents of the Pacha, the chief of the caravan," said Rashid, pointing to the big green tents with gold crescents on their tops. The Pacha's tents occupied the chief place right in the middle of the square.

"The Pacha rides in a splendid litter swung between two beautiful horses, and those must be his dromedaries yonder with the rich trappings," said Rashid, who could explain all this to his little companions, because each year he had seen the caravan arrive and depart, always with the same magnificence and splendour.

It is the religious duty of all good Mohammedans, as the followers of the Great Prophet are called, to make at least one pilgrimage to Mecca, the capital city of Arabia, called the "Holy City."

For this reason every year great caravans from far and near journey across Arabia carrying thousands of pilgrims to Mecca.

"See! see! I do believe there is Nawara," cried Fatimah, "there, just by the big tent."

"Yes, it is she," said Hamid, "and there is the old merchant, too."

With one accord the three children ran down into the square, dodging under camels and around tents, until at last they got to where Nawara was standing. The little girl was so astonished to see her friends of the desert that for a moment she could say nothing. Then she threw her arms around Fatimah, crying out how glad she was to see her again.

"But, Nawara, what are you doing here?" asked Fatimah.

"Grandfather is going to make the pilgrimage to the Holy City, and we are going with the caravan because it is safer," said Nawara, in her little wise way. "Then, too, grandfather will be able to sell his wares to the pilgrims."

The old merchant now joined them and was as pleased to see them again as was his little granddaughter. He had already put on the special dress that pilgrims wear, of white cloth with red stripes, and carried a big rosary of beads at his belt. When he told them that the caravan would stay there until the next day at evening, the children said that Nawara must stay with them until all was ready for the departure. So Nawara went to the great house with Fatimah. Later the old merchant came, too, and Rashid's mother gave them a nice supper. They all sat around a big tray filled with good things to eat, while Nawara told the children of all that had happened to her since they had parted in the desert.

All the next day the young folks waited for the sound of the cannon, which was to be the signal for the caravan to start. Every few minutes one or the other of the boys would rush into the house, saying that the gun had gone off and the camels were going; but it proved each time a false alarm, and Fatimah had just told Nawara to make up her mind to stay another night when the old merchant's servant came rushing in to say that the head of the caravan had already started and was just then passing out the great gate. So once more Nawara had to part from her kind little friends.

The children ran up on top of the house, and for a long time they could see the big caravan winding over the hills and through the plantations of palm-trees.

"Father, can't we go out to the palm groves to-day to see the men gather the dates? Many of the children of the city are going," begged Rashid.

"Yes," said Rashid's father. "I have no doubt but that all you young folks will be fighting together in no time, and there will be more stones gathered than dates. Remember what happened last week." So saying, the Sharif sat back on the divan and took another pull at his long pipe.

Rashid hung his head and tried to look sorry; but his eye twinkled when he thought of the wild scrimmage with sticks and stones that had taken place between the boys of the town and the boys outside the walls. He had fought on the side of the city boys; and, of course, Hamid, though he was of the desert himself, sided with him. There was always great jealousy between these two clans of boys, and they were all the time carrying war into each other's territory; but, after all, not much damage was done on either side beyond some bruised heads and a few broken sticks.

"Thou hast become quite a fighter since thy life in the 'Black Tents,'" said his father; "but if Ali will go along to keep thee from getting into mischief, thou mayst go with thy little friends." Ali said that he would go, and they ran to saddle their ponies.

"How am I to go?" asked Fatimah.

"Oh, thou canst ride with me," said Hamid, like the good brother that he was; and Ali put her up on Zuleika behind Hamid. Away they trotted out of the great gate toward the large groves of palm-trees which surround Medina.

The road was lively with parties of children who, like themselves, were going to the palm groves; for it was the season when the Bedouin farmers cut down the great bunches of dates, and every one, especially the children, made a regular picnic of it. All the children of the city, apparently, were hurrying along, some on horseback and many more on foot, all bent on having a good time.

Just behind our young people came some children riding on donkeys, trying their best to make their little donkeys keep up with the desert ponies of the boys.

Hamid looked back at them and sang out:

"The riding of a horse is an honour to the rider

And joyful is his face;

But the mule is a dishonour

And the donkey a disgrace."

Then Rashid began to laugh. This made the little donkey boys very angry. Off they jumped from their donkeys, and were picking up stones to throw at Rashid and his friends, while Ali threatened them with his stick.

"No wonder father sent me with you to look after you," said Ali, shaking his finger at Hamid and Rashid as they rode on laughing, "if you are bound to get into mischief as early in the day as this."

"But all the same no Bedouin boy would ride a donkey or a mule for anything," said Hamid.

"That is quite true among you desert people," said Ali; "but these town and farmer folk don't care on what they ride so long as they do not have to walk."

Now they had come to a large grove of palm-trees, and near one of the trees was a man standing with a rope in his hand.

"Let us stop here," said Ali, calling out to Rashid; "there is a man going to climb up to the top of a tree now."

The children jumped quickly off their horses and joined the group of people under the trees watching the man.

He had tied one end of the rope around his waist and had passed it around the slim trunk of the tree, attaching the other end also to his waist. With this rope holding him well up against the tree-trunk, he began to climb by holding on to the rough bark wherever he could get a hold for as much as one of his toes, at the same time bracing himself against the strong rope which held him.

"I should not like to do that," said Rashid.

"I wonder that he does not get giddy and fall," said Fatimah.

But the man went up easily, though he had a long way to climb. Like most date-palms, the tree was very tall, and the leaves and fruit all grew together on the very tip-top of the great stem or trunk. It was, as Hamid said, "just like the bunch of feathers on the end of his spear."

When the man finally did reach the bunch of dates, it was quite a job to cut through the big stem, which was nearly as large around as his arm.

"Isn't that a big bunch?" said Hamid, as the man lowered the great golden-coloured dates to the ground.

"Yes," said Rashid, "but look, there must be some larger bunches still, for some are tied up to keep them from breaking off their stems."

The women and children were collecting the gathered dates and packing them in skins and boxes and baskets to be sent away to the markets; but the dried dates that we so often eat are left much longer on the trees to ripen and grow sugary.

"Oh, Hamid, thou and Fatimah must have a 'necklace of sham' to wear! All the children have them!" said Rashid, who had been exploring the garden and had come running quickly back. "There is a woman making them now."

The woman was threading dates on a string and then dipping them into boiling water so that they would keep their pretty golden colour. Then she put them aside in the sun to dry.

Rashid bargained with the woman for three of the necklaces at once.

"It brings one good luck to wear a necklace of the dates of Medina," said the woman as she hung the strings of dates around the children's necks; "and thou must not eat them as this naughty one here has just done." She frowned at her own little girl, who stood by sobbing because her mother had just given her a box on the ear for eating half of her new necklace.

The children had a jolly time helping to pick the dates and pack them, though likely there was more play than work. And they all ate so many dates it was a wonder that they were not ill.

At sundown they rode back to the town, chaffing and laughing with everybody they met along the road. When they got home, hot and tired, Rashid's mother gave them a lovely drink made of the juice of fresh pomegranates, cooled in the snowy ice which was brought down to the city each night from the neighbouring mountains.

"Do you know why the letter 'O' is on every date stone?" asked Rashid that evening as he and Hamid were sitting in the courtyard playing checkers with date stones, while Fatimah sat watching the progress of the game. They often occupied themselves thus in the cool of the evening after supper.

"I have never seen the 'O;' where is it?" asked Hamid, carefully looking at a date stone as if he was only seeing one for the first time.

"There it is," said Rashid, who showed him a tiny round ring on one side of the date stone. "It is said that when our great Prophet first ate of the fruit of the date-palm, he exclaimed: 'Oh! what a fine fruit!' Ever since the letter 'O' has been found on every date stone."

Hamid and Fatimah began looking closely at every date stone they could find; and, sure enough, on every one of them there was a tiny letter "O." You will always find it there, too, if you look for it.

But the young people did not always play. In the early mornings and cool evenings Rashid and Hamid went to school in one corner of the great Mosque. Here the pupils sat in rows on mats, or lounged about on the floor. Before each pupil was a little wooden stand, on which lay a big book from which they shouted out their lessons in a loud voice. They made such a noise that one wonders how they could learn anything at all.

The other children called Hamid the little "Sheik" and often they would forget all about lessons while they listened to his stories about the great desert. Meantime Fatimah was learning how to make many nice new dishes in the big kitchen at home, or she sat with her mother in the women's part of the house, learning how to sew like little city girls.

But, in spite of these happy days spent by the desert folk with the "People of the Walls," the little Bedouins began to long for the great wide desert and its life of freedom. Soon the end of their visit came; one day the little caravan could be seen making its way homeward to their own country far beyond the plain which came up to the city walls.

The first news that Hamid sent Rashid after he got home to the "Black Tents" was about the robber chief. His band had paid a ransom for him and he had been given his liberty, after he had promised solemnly not to attempt to rob or kill again. You must know that a promise made in the "Black Tents" is never broken.

The interchange of visits between Hamid and Rashid occurred regularly each year. Rashid learned of the ways of the dwellers in the "Black Tents;" and gained in health and strength until even Hamid was not his superior in hunting or the rougher games of the plains. Hamid, on the other hand, learned of the life in the Great City, and profited much from the loving companionship of his little friend among the "People of the Walls." Fatimah, too, shared in the happy visits and grew to be called "the beautiful daughter of the Sheik, wise with the wisdom of both desert and city."

THE END.